My First Book of
NURSERY RHYME
FRIENDS
by Diane Stortz

Illustrated by
Kathy Bosch

Little Bo Peep
has lost her sheep,
and doesn't know
where to find them.

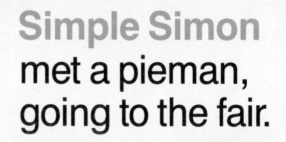

Simple Simon
met a pieman,
going to the fair.

Humpty Dumpty sat on a wall, Humpty Dumpty had a great fall.

Little Boy Blue, come blow your horn, the sheep's in the meadow, the cow's in the corn.

Jack and **Jill** went up the hill to fetch a pail of water.

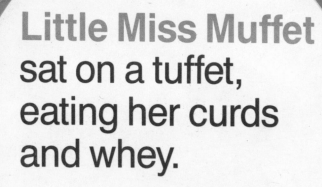

Little Miss Muffet
sat on a tuffet,
eating her curds
and whey.

Old Mother Hubbard went to the cupboard to get her poor dog a bone.

Peter Piper
picked a peck
of pickled peppers.

Diddle, diddle, dumpling, my son **John**, went to bed with his stockings on.

Little Tommy Tucker sang for his supper.

Mary had a
little lamb,
its fleece was
white as snow.

Old King Cole was a merry old soul, and a merry old soul was he.